Her Sister's Man

by

Kandi Silvers

Chapter One

She is really stunning.

Justin Monet glanced at his future sister-in-law Emily across the large dining room table. Beside her was her boyfriend Steve. Sitting next to Justin was his future bride and Emily's sister Portia—his future wife. Though lately, he started to wonder if maybe....

You can't ditch your fiancée for her sister. It's poor taste, and you'll look like an ass.

Logic reasoned but did little to comfort him. Emily's dark gaze turned from the conversation Steve and her father were involved in and cast him a sideways glance and a smile. He couldn't control his grin as she turned away.

"They make a good couple," Portia commented quietly next to him.

"Who?" he asked, focusing on the woman next to him.

Her lips curled up at the edges. "Emily and Steve. I hope he marries her."

Justin stole another look to where Steve was still in deep conversation with the Carter matriarch. Nope. He just couldn't picture Steve and

Emily together long-term. The situation seemed off though they'd been together for over a year.

Or I'm jealous.

"They aren't a perfect couple like you and me," Portia whispered.

He turned to Portia and stared into her bright blue eyes. She was everything a man could want. Only…

"I want to make a toast," Audrey Carter announced and stood opposite the table from her husband. "I'm so glad Portia was lucky to finally meet someone as wonderful as Justin. After being together for three years and officially engaged for two months, I'm glad we could come together with Hilary and Ron Monet as one happy family."

He darted a glance over to his parents, who were focused on Audrey and grinning like fools. The only one at the table not smiling was Emily. She stared in the direction of her mother, but her gaze fell far away and revealed she was lost in thought.

"So let's lift our glasses and toast the wonderful couple."

Glasses lifted, and he turned to Portia and placed a kiss on her lips.

"I'd like to say a few words." Steve stood and lifted his glass toward Justin and Portia. "I figured now would be a good time to make the occasion even more joyful."

Emily turned to Steve, and something unreadable flickered in her dark gaze as she blinked at her boyfriend. "Emily and I have decided to get married."

Her dark, long lashes parted wide, and surprise registered on her pretty face. Her plump full lips pursed together for a fleeting second, then curled into an insincere smile as the congratulations from everyone filtered around them.

"Trust Emily to try and compete with me," Portia breathed.

Justin darted a glance at his future wife, slightly taken aback by her comment. He wasn't sure why it bothered him. She'd made passing remarks similar in the past. "I don't think it's like that."

Her brows furrowed, and she acted as if he were crazy. "Of course, it's like that. She's always been jealous of me."

He glanced over to where Steve and Emily sat. Her sister had no reason to be jealous. She was tall, curvy in all the right spots, with doe-like eyes and long lashes most women would kill for. Her pretty face was framed by dark waves that fell past her shoulders with streaks of deep red and honey highlights. Not to mention she was a brilliant graphic designer and doing well for herself.

Steve was again talking to her father, and Emily stared at her wine glass as if it were the most fascinating object in the room. Beside him, Portia and her mother started rattling on about bridal dresses. He was about to turn away when Emily's gaze met his. This time there was no smile, quite the contrary. Sadness darkened her rich deep brown eyes.

He knew why tonight wasn't sitting right. There were two things. One, he was jealous of Steve, and secondly, Justin realized he was marrying the wrong sister.

And there's nothing I can do.

Chapter Two

Since dinner was almost over, Emily had to excuse herself from the table. Steve didn't even take a moment's pause from talking to her father and instead kept discussing his political campaign. Her stomach hurt, and she was starting to get a tension headache. She couldn't decide what was worse, seeing Portia and Justin together as well engaged or Steve as a complete jerk and making that ridiculous announcement that wasn't even true.

I don't want to marry him. Maybe for a whole five minutes at one time, but not now.

She knew why and it had everything to do with her sister's fiancé. When she was a teenager, she'd always wished she was more like Portia, who was eighteen months older than her. By the time she was twenty, Emily knew what she wanted, liked who she was, and knew Portia would always be Portia. Beautiful and spoiled to the core.

Everything had come easy for her.

She paused in front of the mirror in the hallway and realized she was jealous of Portia. Her sister may be beautiful, but she was vain and selfish. Emily took in her appearance on the reflective surface and sighed. She glanced away and wondered if she slipped outside to the garden if anyone would even notice she was gone.

Steve won't. His head is too far up dad's ass.

Looking back at how things had been recent with the campaign season starting to fire up, she knew where Steve's priorities were. His career and how her father's rich and powerful friends could help him to congress.

"Emily!" Portia entered the hall from the dining room and walked toward her. "I'd like a word with you."

Do I dream of your fiancé? Why yes, Portia, I usually have my vibrator in my hand.

She forced her lips into a smile. "About what?"

"I want you to know I forgive you for announcing your engagement at my dinner to celebrate my marrying Justin."

She blinked and studied her sister. "I didn't announce anything. Steve did."

"Right," Portia nodded her head. "Well, I forgive him too. I know how hard it is for you."

Emily didn't understand and narrowed her gaze. "How hard what is?"

"Having me for a sister. I got the blonde hair, the blue eyes, and the petite frame. You ended up with brown hair and eyes. Plus, you got stuck with being tall and buying jeans with a longer than normal inseam." She patted Emily's knee. "I was the cheerleader and popular, and now I'm marrying

Justin, who is rich, good-looking, and successful. Steve is a great guy. You could have done worse."

Her temper kicked up a notch. Emily knew her sister was vain, but tonight Portia was pushing her usually high vanity bar a few notches closer to the moon. "Steve is a great guy."

Just not great enough to spend the rest of my life with.

"Oh, I know, and he is amazing in bed, but he doesn't make as much money as Justin or have the same family prestige."

Her full lips parted in shock. There were so many things wrong in her sister's single sentence; she didn't even know where to begin. "How do you know he is amazing in bed?"

Good yes. Great on occasion. Amazing—not so far.

Her sister winced, and she scrunched her nose. "I dated him a few times a couple years back."

"Right." The single word fell off Emily's tongue, making her even more upset. "You've been with Justin for three years."

Portia grinned and glanced at her giant engagement ring. "I know." She then met Emily's gaze. "I dated Steve briefly when I didn't think Justin would ever get serious about me and ask me to marry him. I had to keep possibilities open." She batted her lashes. "Besides, we know I'm never single for long."

Because you haven't broken up with one before you start screwing another.

She remained quiet since she was in no mood

to argue with her sister. She would undoubtedly say something she'd regret. It would be the truth, but that wasn't the point.

Portia shrugged. "I'm surprised Steve never told you."

"No, it never came up." She was still stunned by the revelation.

"I can imagine. Probably for the best. Steve most likely didn't want you to feel like you were getting hand-me-downs or that you were second best."

She didn't know how to respond. Emily was more upset that her sister cheated on Justin than over the fact she slept with Steve first.

What the hell is wrong with me?

Her stomach hurt. She needed air.

"There are my girls. We're going to be having tea and coffee in the living room," her mom announced as she darted a look between her two daughters. "Is everything okay?"

"Perfect," Portia replied. "I better find that hunky man of mine." She walked down the hall toward the large living room.

Her mother's gaze rested on her, and her brows dipped with concern. "Are you feeling okay?"

"Fine," she lied. "I just feel a bit warm. I need a bit of air."

"Well, don't be long; dessert will be brought in shortly."

Emily nodded and slowly maneuvered toward the back door of the kitchen. She tugged one of the large French doors and stepped onto the patio.

Inhaling deeply, she hoped the cooler autumn air would cleanse her troubled mind and remove some weight settling on her chest.

The door opened behind her, and she turned to Steven. He pulled her into his arms and grabbed her ass, pulling her toward him. “I’ve been looking for you.” His hands slipped under her skirt, and instead of being aroused, her temper hit full force from his stunt earlier. Looking over Steve’s shoulder, she spotted Justin walking around the corner of the house.

Her sister’s fiancé halted, and his gaze settled where Steve’s hands slowly inched her skirt up. Anger, hurt, and emotions she denied boiled to the surface. She pulled away from Steve as he leaned in to kiss her and glared at him. “Don’t touch me,” she whispered in a heated tone.

“What is your problem?” he asked, blinking in disbelief.

“How could you make that announcement at Portia’s dinner?”

“You agreed to marry me. I figured your father and everyone should know.” His dark eyes studied her. “What the hell has been your problem lately?”

Oh, so many things....

“Stop licking my father’s ass. Politics comes first with you, and I come second.” She shook her head as Justin again disappeared around the corner. “We’ll talk about it later.”

“I can’t spend the night. I have an early meeting.”

She stared at the man in front of her. "I never invited you, nor have I for the last three weeks."

"Yeah, I know, and a man has needs." There was something in his tone she didn't like.

Knowing he'd never mentioned screwing her sister just pissed her off further. "Get in the house. I'll be there in a minute. It'll give you more time to lick my father's shoes."

Steve shook his head and stormed into the house.

Emily sighed and stared up at the night sky. Never did she think her life would be this miserable. Just a year ago, she had everything figured out. Now she was plain sad.

"Don't marry him."

Emily turned and blinked at Justin. She hadn't even heard him approach. Right, because she'd been thinking about him. "What? I thought you liked Steve?"

"I do. Just not for you." His blue-grey eyes darkened, and his expression became unreadable. She waited for him to add more—to say anything, but he didn't. Instead, he studied her intently.

"Justin...." Why did he have to stare at her like that? What was running through his gorgeous head? Why did she get weak in the knees when she was around him? That question was better left unanswered. More so, why was he marrying her dumbass sister? Right, Portia was blonde and beautiful.

"You didn't look like a woman who was

overjoyed and happy when Steve made the announcement at the table." His tone carried an undercurrent usually associated with his temper. Not that she'd seen him angry often over the last few years, but the few times she had…yeah, the trace of emotion coating his words was reminiscent. "Come on, Emi, what's going on?"

"It's a long story and a boring one."

"Actually, when you tell a story, it's never boring. You're animated." Justin shrugged and smiled. "I couldn't help but overhear the conversation. I can't picture you as a politician's wife. You have way too much grit."

Her heart raced a little faster, and she nodded. "True." She needed to change the subject. "So, I talked to your friend Tristan and looked at the website for his bar. It has great potential, but I can see where he needs the help."

"I know it'll be a success, and I actually have a couple investors wanting to step in, but it needs work and a better location."

"Well, I told him I'd do it for free. I can build a rocking website blindfolded, and I'm happy to help. Besides, he can put the money to other things."

Justin studied her for a minute. "That's really nice of you."

She shrugged. "I'm happy to do it." Her stomach fluttered, and she hated herself for the thoughts running through her mind. "Other than my dad, you're the only one that calls me Emi."

The California wind rose up and teased the dark

strands of his hair. "It suits you. Drive's Portia nuts when I do."

Good. Let it.

She didn't delve into her emotions. Emily had more significant problems currently. Like Steve. "Speaking of which, you better get in there before my sister throws a fit."

He paused, then nodded. His expression became unreadable. "Are you coming in?"

She shook her head. "Not yet. I need another moment or two."

Justin nodded his head and pulled open the door. "Okay, I'll see you inside."

Emily nodded and waited for the door to close. When the latch clicked, she exhaled the breath she'd been holding. Emily couldn't keep going like this, keep pretending, and everything about Justin seemed different tonight. Maybe she was different because one thing was evident in her mind.

I want my sister's fiancé.

Chapter Three

Justin went from liking Steve to resenting him in a matter of moments. He'd never been the jealous sort, never had a reason to be. However, now Justin knew what the emotion was firsthand. He'd meant every word when he told Emily he didn't think she should marry Steve. The image of her resisting her boyfriend as he ran his hands over her smooth, silky skin played out in his mind. So many times over the last year, Justin wanted to touch her, but he was taken.

He glanced around the room and didn't see Portia. Now, where did she go? She'd been a completely different person for the last couple of weeks. Then again, so was he. He coveted her sister.

Could he be a bigger asshole?

Probably.

Portia entered the room from the hallway and sat down beside him. In her hand was her cell phone, and she glanced up at him. "Sorry about that, Lucy called."

His brows furrowed, and he ignored Emily's laughter from across the room, where she talked quietly with his mother and grandmother. "Is everything okay?"

Her blue eyes filled with sadness. "She and Julio had another fight, and I guess he went to his brother's, and she is a horrible mess."

Justin nodded in understanding. Lucy had a turbulent relationship with her boyfriend. He could only remember meeting him in passing and doubted he'd exchanged more than a half dozen sentences with the man in the last three years. "Is she going to be okay?"

She shrugged. "I don't know. This time it seems serious. I'm thinking of going to see her after we leave here."

He could understand that Lucy seemed to need Portia a lot these days. That wasn't necessarily a bad thing. Maybe one day, Portia might need Lucy. "Sure thing."

"Well, we'd best be going," Steve announced. "I have an early meeting in the morning, so I'm going to take Emily home and call it a night."

"You live out toward the valley, Portia and I can take Emily home," Justin spoke up before thinking it through. "If it's okay with you?"

"That would be great," Emily responded before Steve could even part his lips to reply. "Thank you." She turned to her boyfriend. "It'll save you from having to double back."

"Thanks, man, I appreciate it," Steve told him with a nod.

Portia touched Justin's sleeve. "If Steve is going

right home, he can drop me off at Lucy's on his way."

Alone with Emily? Hell, not good.

He took in the hopeful expression in Portia's blue eyes and found himself agreeing. "Yeah, it makes sense." He glanced back at Steve and Emily but caught the unhappy expression on Emily's face before she turned away. "I'd appreciate it," he told the other man.

"Not a problem." His gaze fell on Portia. "Are you ready?"

"Yes." She stood, leaned in, and kissed Justin's lips briefly. "I'll call you later."

"Sounds good." He knew that she'd probably end up drinking wine, talking till all hours, lose track of time, and then stumble in the door sometime by early morning.

His fiancée hurried toward the door with Steve and left after both said their goodbyes. A small amount of relief washed over him. A million thoughts ran through his head, and he shoved them aside to focus on one. He'd be alone with Emily.

Maybe I should talk to her.

Then what? He'd come across as a jerk. He darted a glance at her. "Whenever you're ready."

She smiled weakly. "I'm ready now."

He stood and walked over to his parents and grandmother. "I'm going to give Emily a ride home. Steve is taking Portia over to her friend's house."

His mother nodded, and his granny rolled her eyes and then focused on him. "Well, make sure Emily gets inside safe. She's such a nice girl."

Justin couldn't control his smile as he remembered mentioning she would build Tristan's club's website for free. "That she is. Listen, I'll come to see you this week." He leaned in, kissed the older woman's cheek, then turned to his dad. "Have a good night."

His father grinned and nodded. "You too, son."

Doubtful.

He smiled, then waved goodbye to her parents, escaped the Carter home into the night, and walked her down the walk to his waiting car on the drive. Justin reached in his pocket, withdrew the key, then hit the remote before glancing at Emily standing by the vehicle. He reached for the handle and paused. "I never got a chance to tell you, but you look really nice tonight."

Her eyes sparkled in the reflection of the lights, and her lips turned into a smile. "Thank you." Justin couldn't miss the surprise in her voice or the expression on her face.

They stood there a moment and just stared at each other in silence. It took every ounce of his being not to lean in and kiss Emily's full mouth—if anything, to see if they were as soft as they looked. Justin swallowed hard and opened the door for her. She slid in, and he shut it behind her. He walked around to the driver's side and swore it would be the longest twenty minutes of his life.

For most of the ride, Emily remained quiet and stared out the passenger window. At every stop light, he stole a glance her way through the rearview mirror. Her features completely contrast Portia's but are no less beautiful. Actually, in some ways, she was prettier than her sister. He could tell she was lost in thought and wondered if she'd open up. Whatever was on her mind troubled her, and he guessed it had to do with Steve.

He pulled his vehicle into the drive and turned off the ignition. "You've been out of sorts all night," he finally voiced.

She turned to him and smiled. "Yeah, I have a lot on my mind."

Justin nodded and then opened the car door. "I'll walk you up."

He walked around and opened her door and watched as her long, tanned legs stepped out of the vehicle. He followed her to the front step and waited for her to unlock the door. She turned the handle and blinked up at him. "Did you want to come in for a minute?"

"Yeah, I'd like that. Are you going to tell me what's bothering you?"

Hesitation illuminated her face beneath the front light, but she nodded, then pushed open the door. Justin closed it behind them and followed her up the stairs, noticing how her dress curved over her shape. His gaze lingered on her hips, and he couldn't help but wonder what they'd feel like beneath his hold. Emily flipped on a light, kicked off her shoes, and then turned and faced him. "How honest do you want me to be?"

He closed the distance between them and

studied her. “Very honest, there isn’t anything you can’t tell me.”

A fleeting unreadable expression crossed her face before it disappeared as quickly as it had surfaced. “I was just wondering what it would have been like if I’d met you before Portia.”

His heart slammed to a stop. All night, she’d been thinking about him. “I don’t know.” Justin studied the beauty before him. “I might have an answer, but I need to find something out first.”

“Anything.” Her big brown lashes batted. “What is it?”

Chapter Four

Emily couldn't describe the expression on Justin's handsome face. He remained silent a moment, and she wondered if she'd been too blunt or bold and put him in an awkward spot.

"I want to know if you'll forgive me."

Confused now, she shook her head. "For what?"

He lowered his head to hers, and her lashes fluttered shut. His warm breath teased against her lips, sending heat through her entire body before his mouth covered hers in a kiss.

Emily's knees buckled, and she dropped her clutch. Her hands rested on his shoulders while he circled her waist with his hands. His tongue slid across her lower lip, then nibbled, forcing her to gasp. He tasted divine as he entered her mouth, and she slid her arms around his neck. His hands slid from her lower back and cupped her ass. Her breasts came against his solid chest, and she moaned against his tongue when his arousal pressed against her pelvis.

Justin deepened the kiss. He hiked up her skirt until his palms heated the flesh of her backside. He caressed her hips and dipped one hand between her legs to where she was growing damp with desire. His finger slid across the front of her lace thong, and her knees buckled. With one strong arm and a couple of steps, he eased her back against the wall. Wasting no time, he dipped his fingers beneath the panty and pushed one long finger inside her.

His growl crashed against her lips as he started working in and out of her. Her nipples hardened, and she wanted more than anything to touch him. Their mouths stayed locked as she slipped her hands to the waistband of his pants and undid the belt, button and zipper. Justin slipped a second finger inside her. Emily shoved her hand into the waist of his boxers and caressed the skin of his rock-hard cock before curling eager fingers around his length. A moan escaped him as she glided a finger over the tip, moist with pre-cum. Feeling her effect on him aroused her further, and Emily struggled to breathe and not break the kiss. Her hand slid from the tip of Justin's dick down. She soon fell into a steady stroke that matched his fingers working in and out of her.

The hand not stroking him lifted and laced through his hair. Emily's tongue continued mating with his, and Justin's fingers picked up speed. Pressure and heat built in her belly, and her hold around him tightened. A feral growl escaped him as she ran her fingers down to the base, then slid across his sac before gliding back up to the tip. His thumb grazed her clit as his fingers still worked her wet walls. Her body stiffened. She pulled out of the kiss as her head thumped the wall, and her shoulders trembled. Her pussy clamped around his fingers and coated them with his release.

"God, Emi!" Justin rasped, and his cock pulsed beneath her grasp. She covered the head with her shaking palm as his climax left in a ribbon of hot release. The pleasure washing over his handsome face was the hottest thing Emily had ever seen. Her walls twitched around his fingers deep inside, and she forced a small breath into his lungs.

Justin met her gaze and scanned her face. "Incredible," he breathed and softly brushed his lips against hers while neither pulled away.

"It was," she whispered.

A small smile tugged his firm and puffy lips into a grin. "No, in answer to your question." He inhaled a couple ragged breaths. "It would have been incredible if I'd met you first."

She nodded in agreement, and sadness filled her heart.

"This…this was amazing—amazing and unexpected."

The ramifications of what she'd just done hit her full force. Never had she ever cheated on a boyfriend.

She swallowed and carefully removed her hand. She eased away from Justin before she decided to take him down to the bedroom. Christ! Full-on sex would not help things right about now and make the situation worse. She walked to the hall bathroom, washed her hand, and grabbed a cloth. Her legs were shaky, but she walked back to where he stood.

His gaze met hers as he took the washcloth. "I'm so sorry."

She shook her head and resisted the urge to cry. "I think I should be the one apologizing. I...wasn't expecting...:" What could she say? "I don't want problems between you and Portia."

A solemn expression crossed his handsome face, and he debated. As to what, Emily had no idea. "I shouldn't have kissed you, but I needed to know."

She didn't trust her voice, so she simply nodded once.

"I better go," he whispered, but the regret in his voice wasn't hard to miss as he passed her back the cloth and tucked himself back into his pants. His blue-grey eyes carried grief when he again met her gaze. "If you need anything, call me."

"I will," she assured. With a shaking hand, she touched Justin's cheek, then stretched up and placed a kiss where her hand had been. "You too," she braved to whisper.

Justin nodded and walked toward the stairs. She didn't dare turn and see him leave, or two things would happen. One, she'd beg him not to go, or two, start to cry.

Emily waited until the door shut and bent down to pick up her clutch. She reached inside her purse, withdrew her phone, and realized she didn't feel much guilt for what happened. In fact, if Justin had wanted more, she would have gladly given it—all night long or until both were totally spent.

She wondered if the events were because she was angry at Portia and Steve and if Steve would give her sister more than a ride to an upset friend. No. The truth was more disturbing; she truly cared about Justin.

Oh, my god, I think I love him.

Emily stared at her phone and then started dialing Steve's number. Enough was enough.

Chapter Five

Emily's first twenty-four hours blurred into one significant memory. Though she functioned, she didn't recall anything except what she'd done with Justin. Now she sat in front of Portia's nail salon so she could pick her up and meet their mom at the wedding planner's boutique. Her sister had said she'd be at work but, for some reason, hadn't been. None of the women, including Lucy, had seen her since yesterday.

Again, she dialed her sister's cell, which went straight to voice mail.

Her stomach knotted.

The last thing she wanted to do was help Portia plan a wedding when she had feelings for the groom-to-be. She glanced around and wondered how much longer she should wait. Across the street, a grey sports car stopped, and a guy got out. From the passenger side, her sister emerged.

What the hell?

The guy walked over to Portia, wrapped his arms around her sister's waist, and pulled her into a lip-locking kiss. His hands cupped her ass, and her sister ground her hips against him. The knot in Emily's stomach turned to stone.

She knew damn well the guy wasn't Justin.

The little bitch.

A weight settled on her chest as her sister stepped out of the guy's arms and hurried across. Her sister didn't even notice her, and Emily honked the horn. Her temper kicked up, and any remorse for what she had done with Justin evaporated.

Never to be seen again.

Her sister smiled and waved, then quickly climbed in the car. "Sorry, I'm late. I had to drop some stuff off at the post office for the girls at the salon."

Emily turned to her sister. "Don't lie to me. God, do you really think I'm that stupid?" As the seconds ticked by, she became angrier. "What is running through your blonde head other than air?"

Portia's expression held surprise then her blue gaze narrowed. "Don't be a bitch. Henry works at the coffee shop next to the salon. We're friends. Now let's go, mom is waiting, and we're going to be late."

"First off, don't boss me around. I'm not one of the boy toys you fuck. Second, what I witnessed was more than friends. It's friends with benefits."

"For cripes sake, don't be such a prude. I'm young, beautiful, and have needs."

If Justin is that good with his fingers, what the hell needs could she have unfulfilled by the rest of him?

Her sister sighed. "Spare me the oh-my-god! You're cheating speech." Her sister scowled. "What are you going to do? Tell mom and dad or worse, Justin?" Her sister laughed maliciously. "No one will believe you."

She blinked at the other woman. "Why won't they?"

"For real?" Her sister blinked at her as if she were stupid. "Because you'll look like you are trying to cause problems because you're jealous I'm getting married and getting all the attention."

"But you *are* cheating on Justin." Her heart sank because her sister was a complete idiot.

"So, he's been weird lately, and I have no intention of being faithful until I'm good and ready. Now for cripes sake, let's go." Her sister folded her arms and looked ahead as if the conversation was over.

There were a hundred things Emily wanted to say to her sister but instead held her tongue. She slowly peeled away from the curb, becoming more upset and angrier with every rotation of the wheels.

"Are you going to speak to me?" Portia finally asked.

Her patience frayed further. "Not unless I have to."

"Justin doesn't always satisfy me. I mean, he's good and all, but even your ex-boyfriend Steve was better in bed." She sighed and started digging in her purse. "I still can't believe you two broke up. I was hoping you'd actually get married."

There was something in her tone that sent Emily's senses on alert. "What does it matter to you if I married him or not?" She stopped the car in front of the wedding planner's shop and turned to her sister.

Portia stared at her and smiled. "I just thought it would make things better." Her sister opened the car door. "Come on, we're almost half an hour late."

"No, go by yourself. I have things to do other than you plan a wedding when you can't even be faithful to the man you are supposed to be marrying."

"Give it a rest. Not everyone is a frigid prude like you."

Her resolve started to dissipate. "Do you even love Justin?"

"I'm marrying him. He's rich and really hot. Not to mention successful. Yeah, I love him."

She sat speechlessly. "Tell mom I have a migraine. Now get out."

Portia glanced back and again scowled. "I know you're doing this because, as usual, you're jealous." She slammed the car door before Emily could respond.

"No, you stupid bitch," she whispered to the empty car. "I'm in love with your fiancé, and you don't even know the meaning of the word."

Chapter Six

Five days since Justin left Emily's, he still couldn't shake what had happened. He had never cheated on a girlfriend in his life, yet he chose to do it with his fiancée's sweet but very sexy sister. Usually, Justin would talk to his dad, but this time, he couldn't. However, he needed to talk about what was running through his head. He came to the stop light and thought about Portia. She'd barely been home, and when she was, it was never for long, or she showered and went to bed. Fine by him. He was glad since he didn't want to have sex with her and think about Emily. The light changed, and he continued down the street and saw the lights to Tristan and Trevor's nightclub.

Tristan's sports car was parked and turned into the parking lot. Tristan had been his friend since college and always gave him things straight. The other man was like a brother to him, hoping he'd have some advice on how to handle the situation. He knew what he wanted: to call off the wedding. Again though, how bad would it be to start dating the sister?

He turned off the ignition and sat in the car a moment. Tristan knew the truth about Justin and Portia and how he'd almost broken up with her a year ago. He opened the door, unfolded his frame from the luxury car, and walked up to the entrance. He pulled open the door and spotted Tristan immediately behind the bar.

His friend leaned across and smiled at a brunette with her back to the door. He knew the curve of the hips, the long tanned legs under the mini denim skirt, and the streaks running through her hair by heart. He fantasized about them often, especially now he knew what she tasted like and how hard she'd climaxed around his fingers. The memory even now stirred his cock. Every passing second he was grateful his suit coat covered his growing arousal.

Tristan glanced up, and his grin broadened. "Justin, welcome, brother!"

Emily turned, and her face lit up. The entire mouth he knew every detail of and longed to kiss again curled into a smile. He knew then and there —the gesture was solely for him, and her eyes sparkled. She was genuinely happy to see him.

He walked over to the bar and saw Emi's laptop was open. In front of her sat a near-empty glass of red wine, and he glanced at Tristan. "How are things going?"

His friend nodded. "Great, Emily here has some kick-ass ideas for the club."

"She is very good at what she does. One of my

clients used her for a project, and sales skyrocketed."

"Good to know. Can I get you a beer?"

"No, I'm good for now." Justin met the beauty's gaze, and his grin widened. "I didn't see your car."

"Ahh... yes, the traitor that it is wouldn't start, and since Portia wasn't at work or answering her phone, dad dropped me off so I could catch up with Tristan and see the club."

Why wasn't his fiancé at work? He shook it off and added it to his growing list of questions. Instead, he focused on the woman in front of him with light in her eyes. Staring at him as if he'd just hung the moon, especially for her. "Did you need a ride home?"

She blinked and nodded. "If it's not out of the way."

"No, I was just in the neighborhood and thought I'd swing in and say hi, but I can catch up with Tristan later."

Her eyes sparkled. "That would be great. We were pretty much done." She turned to Tristan. "I think I have everything I need." She closed her light and slender laptop and slipped it into her bag. "I'll get some concepts for you over the next couple of days."

"That would be great." He turned to Justin. "Give me a call later or swing back by."

He knew the tone of Tristan's voice.

Tristan either had questions or was interested in Emily. The latter bothered him; maybe it was because she was already taken or because he had feelings for the pretty brunette.

They exited Crossroads and walked to the car. He cast a glance at her and debated. "I was going to see my grandma. Did you have to hurry home, or would you want to go? I know she asked about you the other day."

Emily's footsteps paused, and she glanced up at him. "I'd really like that. I always enjoy talking to her. It's a shame it only seems to be at family get-togethers."

His heart picked up speed, and there was something about the moment. Maybe it was the sincerity in her tone, how happy she'd been to see him, or just how she lit up a room by just being there. Now under the afternoon sun, she looked more beautiful than ever. "All right then," he grinned and walked to the passenger door. Justin scanned her pretty face and met her gaze. "Thank you."

Her brows dipped as if she didn't understand. "For what?"

"Just being you." He opened the car door, and she slid in. Then he walked around and found himself happy he could spend some time with her.

He pulled out of the parking lot and darted a glance her way. "Tristan seemed pleased."

She turned to him and shifted in her seat, exposing more of her legs. The memory of their satin texture beneath his palms as he caressed her came into his mind in full recollection. "He is very nice. I like him and his brother Trevor both. Very hard workers. I'm so glad I can help them out."

"I still can't believe you're doing it for free." It was the truth. He knew how hefty the price tag Emily's work came at, especially since his client had raved she was worth every penny.

Every expensive penny.

"Tristan again offered me money, and I told him not to worry; I work for wine."

Justin chuckled. "What did he say to that?"

"He asked if I wanted red or white."

He couldn't control his grin. His mind shifted to Portia and Tristan. Portia didn't like Tristan, and his friend often remained quiet when her name came up. "I'm glad you two get along."

"Yeah, I should have something ready for him in a week or so. I can fit it around my other clients' work easily enough. So how was your day?"

He wanted to tell her he'd missed her since he'd walked out her door almost a week ago but refrained. She probably wouldn't believe him anyway. "It was good. Work is going great, and I think I picked up another client."

"I think it's great how well you've done professionally. I know how much work and effort it takes to grow in your field." She was quiet for a moment, and he wondered what she was thinking. Finally, she spoke. "I need to stop before we see your grandmother if that's okay?"

He pulled his gaze off the road and turned to the woman sitting in his passenger seat. "Is everything okay?" He focused again on traffic, but not before glancing at her smooth, tanned legs.

"Oh, everything is fine. Didn't you mention some time ago how your grandmother loved lilies? The other night, when we talked, she mentioned she missed her garden since she moved into the care facility. I just want to stop and grab her some flowers."

Jesus!

He saw the light change but went through on the stale amber and only crossed the intersection thoroughly after turning red. Horns honked, and he had to get his head screwed on straight before he killed Emily and himself.

"Yeah, she loves lilies." His words left his mouth in a crisp tone, only they came across harsher than he'd intended.

"If it's too much trouble...."

No. No, it's not...bloody hell.

"No." Justin slammed on his signal light and pulled a sharp right turn into a strip mall where there was a flower shop. What the hell was he doing? Justin brought the luxury car to a stop, threw it in park, turned the vehicle off, and turned in his seat. Where did he even begin?

Emily blinked long lashes, and apprehension dusted across her pretty features. "I didn't mean to put you out. I just thought—"

"Of someone other than yourself?" He finished the sentence. It wasn't what she would say, but it was the blatant truth.

She pulled her full lips between her teeth and

remained quiet.

So many thoughts and feelings swarmed inside his head, and he didn't even know where to begin. "Emi..."

"I can quickly run in if you want to wait in the car." She unfastened her seatbelt. "I won't be long." Her tone resembled that of a lost little girl.

"Wait, please." Justin debated his words, then realized he might implode if he didn't say what he needed to. "In the three years, I've been with your sister. Not once has she ever suggested stopping to get my grandmother flowers."

She tilted her head from side to side. "Well, that's Portia. I'm sure if she—"

"Please, don't make excuses for her." A heavy weight settled on his chest. He clicked the button for his safety belt and reached to her cheek, gently cupping her face in his hand. "You're killing me, Emi. Don't marry Steve. He doesn't deserve you."

A strange expression crossed her features, and her brow furrowed. "I thought Portia would've told you."

"Told me what?" Portia hadn't said a word to him as far as her sister was concerned. What was up with her silent hate-on for Emily?

"I'm not marrying Steve. I broke up with him last week after dinner. Actually, about ten minutes after you left." She sighed and shook her head. "I knew he wasn't what I wanted."

Justin wasn't sure what to say. Why didn't Portia tell him? "I didn't know."

Emily blinked at him, and something flickered in her dark eyes. "Do you ever think about the kiss the other night?"

Kiss? It was a hell of a lot more than a kiss.

His groin tightened. "Yeah, I do. I know it was wrong, but even as I sit here now, I can't help but want to kiss you again."

A small smile tugged her lips into a smile. "We both know it was more than a kiss."

His cock grew hard, remembering how she tasted and her orgasm around his fingers. "I have to say it was one of the most intense moments of my life." He wanted to bury himself inside her and wished he had the other night instead of climaxing in her hand.

Her pretty face twisted into a thoughtful expression. "Well, it'll be our secret, especially since I don't think I've ever cum that hard in my life."

Oh God, you've been with the wrong men.

The thought sobered his senses. Justin wanted Emily in the worst way and to take her higher than the one he'd already given her a week ago. He thought of how hard he'd climaxed from her soft touch and didn't deny he'd be buried deep inside her when Justin released next time.

He debated and then went for honesty. "The only reason I haven't kissed you is that I'm going to want to do a hell of a lot more than taste your mouth and slide a finger or two in you."

Her dark eyes widened, and long dark lashes parted. "I..." She glanced down at her hands twisting in her lap, then turned back. Whatever she was thinking had her in considerable debate. "Don't think less of me."

What the...?

"Why on earth would you say that?" Justin had no idea where that thought came from.

She lifted her gaze and blinked at him. "Because I want you too."

Justin's mouth curled into a grin. "Why don't we grab granny flowers, go see her, then go somewhere and talk."

Emily nodded, then her perfectly arched brows crinkled. "What about Portia?"

Ah, yes...

"She's staying at Lucy's for a couple days. I guess she and her boyfriend had another fight, and this one was even more serious. So Portia is staying with her to make sure she's okay."

An unreadable expression crossed Emily's face, but she didn't look impressed. "Let's grab the lilies and go from there."

Justin nodded and knew it was just a matter before Emily was naked in his arms.

God Help us!

Chapter Seven

Emily walked into her condo and was genuinely happy for the first time in a long time. She'd enjoyed the visit with Justin's granny and genuinely liked the woman. She didn't get her sister, but she hadn't spoken to her since she'd dropped her tramp ass off at the wedding boutique.

"Thank you," Justin spoke from behind her. "You made my grandmother's week with the flowers. It was good to see her that happy."

She turned and took in his appearance. He was so handsome and so sweet to his elderly family. All Tristan could do was tell her what a good friend he'd been over the years. "You're very welcome. I really enjoyed it."

"I could tell." He stepped closer to her, and desire flickered in his gaze. He reached out, captured her wrist in his hand, and tugged her toward him.

Heat coursed through her and her stomach fluttered. The conversation from the parking lot came back to her. She scanned his face, hoping to find an answer to a question she didn't know.

"I can't stop thinking about you," he whispered.

"Emi, I—"

She stretched up and covered his mouth with hers, cutting off whatever else he would say. The instant her lips touched his, he groaned, released her wrist, and circled her waist in his tight hold. She laced her arms around his neck while his tongue entered her mouth. Her fingers entwined in the hair at the back of Justin's neck, and she savored the velvety texture of his tongue as it met hers. Her panty dampened, and her body came alive in his hold.

Justin lifted his mouth from hers, and she met his gaze. "Not here."

Before she could respond, he walked her backward down the hall to her bedroom. "Are you sure about this?" She finally dared to ask.

"More than I've been sure about anything in my life." His arms left her waist, captured the hem of her t-shirt, and pulled it over her head. Nerves fluttered in her stomach. He wouldn't like what he'd see. She wasn't built like her sister. Justin tossed her shirt to the floor and his gaze raked over Emily's breasts tucked into the lace of her bra. "God, you're beautiful."

She didn't doubt him for a second from the desire blazing in his eyes. She reached up, shoved his suit jacket from his shoulders, and felt relieved he wasn't wearing a tie. Emily pulled Justin's shirt from the waist of his pants and slipped her fingers beneath the skin of his stomach. Defined abs met her touch. He had already started unbuttoning his shirt and reclaimed her mouth in a kiss when it fell open.

She shoved the shirt off, hitting the floor where his jacket lay. His hands ran over her arms, grasped them, and pulled her toward his solid, defined torso. Her breasts came against him and her nipples hardened from the heat he radiated. His tongue entered her mouth while his fingers worked the button and zipper of her skirt.

When undone, it fell to the floor. Emily deepened the kiss as his hands caressed her body and down over the flesh of her ass. He cupped the firm, round globes as her fingers made quick work of his belt and pants opening. She slid her fingers over his rock-hard arousal beneath the silk of his boxers and moaned. He ended the kiss and eased her away. Justin removed the remainder of his clothes and stood naked and magnificent in front of her. His cock jutted out, and he captured her with a strong arm and eased her back on the bed. He kissed her lips and neck and coated her collarbone with the same affection.

Her desire grew, and she wiggled as he pressed his stiff cock into her belly. His mouth trailed over her body, and his fingers found the clasp nestled at her cleavage. He unfastened the bra and peeled back the lace. His hot mouth wrapped around one of the peaks, and he gently sucked. Her hips bucked beneath him, and he pressed his length harder against her belly.

"God!" he groaned as he lifted his mouth from her taut nipple and trailed kisses down over her stomach until he reached the top of her thong. His tongue snaked across the top before his teeth and fingers captured the fabric. He gently removed his mouth and stripped the soaked lace from her body.

Justin's gaze roamed over her as she slipped out of her bra and tossed it down. Nothing but carnal desire reflected in his gaze as he stretched his muscled frame over her. His elbows rested on either side of her head, and she shifted beneath him. His dick slid across her wet folds, and her body begged him to thrust inside her.

Neither spoke nor broke the gaze as his tip teased her entrance. Her pussy pulsed in need, and he thrust in as if hearing the silent call.

"Christ!" he breathed as his size filled her completely. "You feel incredible," he rasped, then covered her lips with his in a hot, hungry kiss. She sighed against his tongue as he slowly started working in and out of her. Due to his size, every movement rubbed against her wet walls. She rocked her hips and met his thrusts as her tongue entered his mouth and entwined with his. His pace picked up, and pressure built fast and tight across her abdomen. She moaned against his tongue, which fired him to thrust deeper. The pressure intensified, and her hands slipped to his shoulders as he plunged in and out of her.

A feral groan crashed against her tongue, and her body bucked beneath him. The tight build-up broke, and her body stiffened, lifting her back off the bed before her shoulders trembled and shook her body. Her lips left him, and she wailed as her walls convulsed tightly around his still thrusting cock. Her fingers dug into his shoulders, and his loud grunt filled the room around them. Justin's movements paused as he slid his hands by her head, grasped her arms, and rolled, taking her with him.

Emily loved the feel of her bare skin against his but hoisted herself up, so she straddled his lap where his dick was still buried deep inside her. Emily braced herself against his solid chest and rotated her hips while his strong hands captured and guided her movements. He lifted and met her rhythm as she slowly worked her pussy up and down his length.

Again pressure started to grow in her belly, and his thrusts gained momentum. "Oh, God, Justin." She whimpered as again her body grew higher and tighter with arousal.

His breathing became ragged, and his grip tightened at her hip bones. Justin groaned loudly and thrust harder and deeper than before. "Fuck, yes!" he roared as his cock pulsed. His release emptied inside her, and her shoulders rocked from the intensity of the orgasm ripping through her entire body. As her wet walls grasped him tight, Justin moaned again and milked him with her climax.

She struggled for air and became light-headed. Emily eased herself down and rested her cheek against his wet chest as her entire body quivered from the aftermath. Justin's arms wrapped around her tightly, and he held her against him. Their hearts raced, and she savored the intimacy as they regained their breath.

"Are you okay?" he asked with a husky whisper.

"More than okay," she smiled and lifted her head to meet his gaze.

He lifted a hand and ran it through the strands of her hair while his one arm held her close. "I admit this was even better than I could have imagined or fantasized about."

She smiled, soothed by his words. "This was officially the most intense sex I've ever had."

A lazy grin curled across his mouth. "Emi, I'm just getting started."

Emily couldn't imagine it getting any better than this—unless he was hers and not her sister's.

Chapter Eight

It was past two in the morning when Justin left Emily's. She'd fallen asleep in his arms, and he hated that he had to leave her. His day had been incredible, and he highly doubted there were words to describe how amazing his night had been. It wasn't just the sex. It was the conversation over Chinese and the way he felt when he was with her. She wasn't bored when he talked about work and asked questions. He couldn't remember a night like tonight, even when he and Portia started dating. The two women were nothing alike in appearance and less alike in personality. Instead of heading home, he drove down the street and jumped on the freeway to the next exit. Justin saw the familiar sign to Crossroads and was relieved to see Tristan still here.

He walked into the bar that still had patrons gathered in small groups and a couple at the bar. Tristan met his gaze as soon as he walked in, and his long-time friend shook his head as he approached. "I thought your white-collar ass would be in bed by now."

Justin couldn't fight the grin. "I was in bed or at

least on it for a good portion of the night."

The other man studied him and shook his head. "Come to the office. I'll grab us a beer." He turned to the cooler, withdrew two beers, popped the caps, and led the way to his office.

He shut the door as Tristan parked himself in his chair and motioned to one of the worn ones in front before passing Justin a beer. "Thanks." He sipped from the bottle and met his friend's gaze. "Why are you looking at me like that?"

Tristan shrugged. "Waiting for you to talk." A wicked smile tore across his mouth. "You look good. Disheveled but good. Long night?"

"I had the best and worst night of my life tonight." He thought again of Emily and wished he had just stayed with her. Portia stayed out all night. Would she even notice if he wasn't there? "I cheated on Portia."

"Ah!" his friend lifted his brows. "Seeing I've known you a long time, I know that's a first. You aren't the cheating kind."

"Not until the other night when I kissed someone I shouldn't have, did things get out of hand." He paused. "Take that literally—not metaphorically."

"Wow, and tonight you sealed the deal." The amusement left his friend's voice. "I can see how that would make it the worst night."

Justin sighed. "Pretty much." He again drank some of the beer. "Aren't you going to ask me why it was the best?"

His friend shook his head and smiled. "I don't need to. My money is on a leggy brunette who has got to be the sweetest thing going."

"How did you know?"

"You're kidding, right?" Tristan gulped back from his bottle and ran his tongue over his lips. "I've been here, man, for the last three years I've been here, including last year when you first thought you might have feelings for Emily." He paused and debated. "Did you tell her you almost broke up with Portia because you were falling for her? Hell, I still don't know why you just didn't go for it then."

"She started dating Steve." The truth fell off his tongue. "Only now they've broken up, and she's single. I'm pretty sure I'm engaged to a woman who is cheating on me and has been for a while, and to top it off, I'm falling in love with her sister."

"I hate to disappoint you. You aren't falling in love with her. You've been in love with her for a while." He studied him intently. "I can't tell you what to do, but I know that Emily feels the same way about you. Dude, I have seen you with Portia countless times, and never has the blonde looked at you the way her sister does."

Justin sighed and nodded as he digested Tristan's words. "You're right. I do love Emily."

"So, my friend, what will you do about it?"

I don't know. Can I have perfect or perfection?

Justin's heart broke. He knew the truth and had fought it for so long...he didn't know the truth anymore. "I want Emi...."

Tristan laughed. “I’d thought you’d say that.”

Chapter Nine

Something felt different as Emily walked into her townhouse. Over the last couple of weeks, she was different and officially having an affair with her sister's fiancé. A weight settled over Emily's chest, and she dropped her keys on the table. She darted to one of the chairs with Justin's suit jacket draped over the back.

"Justin?" She called and walked down the hall to her bedroom. Justin's clothes were at the foot of the bed, and he emerged from the bathroom with a towel draped around his waist and looking sexier than hell.

"Hey, I thought you had meetings." He leaned in, kissed her lips, and sat at the bed's edge.

She sighed and kicked off her high heels. "They got canceled, so I swung by crossroads and showed Tristan and Trevor the website. They're thrilled." She thought for a moment. "How did you get in?"

"Hide a key," he confessed and worked his gaze over her bare legs and up over her dress, then looked her in the eyes. Desire blazed in his blue-grey regard. "Come here."

She stepped over to where he sat, and she studied him. "Is everything okay?"

He smiled and nodded. "Yeah, things are fine. I didn't want to go to my place, so I thought I'd come here and surprise you."

Emily couldn't control the grin. "I like this kind of surprise."

"I am going to call off the wedding. I can't keep going like this, pretending to be with Portia when all I want is you." He sighed. "You're incredible, Emi, and I want to be with you."

Justin's words warmed her heart. She'd be glad when the wedding to her sister was officially off, and they could move on from an affair to a relationship. "I'd like that."

His grin broadened, and he slid his hands over the skin of Emily's thighs and underneath the light fabric of her dress until he caressed the flesh of her ass and cupped it in his palms. He tilted his chin, and she bent in to cover his mouth with hers. Heat ignited her body, and she placed her hands on his muscled, damp shoulders.

Justin nibbled her lower lip and slid his tongue across before entering her mouth. His hold on her increased, and he groaned against her tongue. He slid his hands to the top of her satin thong and gently tugged it. The wet fabric teased her skin as it fell to her feet. She stepped out of the underwear and let her hands caress Justin's chest and across his defined and corded abdominal muscles.

His palms slid across to the front, and his

fingers dipped between her legs, already moist with desire. Gently Justin teased the folds and ran the pad of a finger over her clit before lowering to Emily's entrance and penetrating her with his touch. Her hand curled around the top of the towel and undid the fold, so the thick terry fell away.

Emily caressed his belly and lower and discovered his cock thick with arousal. She lifted her lips from his, placed one knee on the bed, and then the other, straddling his hips. Justin removed his finger from inside her, then hiked up her dress as she wrapped a hand around his hardened length, guided it to her entrance, and lowered herself down over him. His head tilted back, and pleasure washed over his handsome face as her velvet sheath captured him.

"God, Emi, you feel incredible."

She smiled wickedly and wiggled her hips, pressing his dick hard against her pussy walls. "So do you."

His hands settled on her bare hips as she rocked her hips back and forth a few times before lifting then lowering herself over him. Her arms laced around his neck, and she worked herself up and down over his arousal. His mouth claimed hers in a carnal kiss, and his tongue thrust inside in search of hers. She bucked her hips and then rotated them in a circle, keeping him deep inside her. He moaned against her tongue, and his hands tightened on her hips and started moving her body.

Pressure built in her pelvis, and she whimpered

from the intensity of his movements rocking her. His pace picked up, and the invisible band deep in her belly grew tighter. Emily lifted her mouth and held him tighter as the band broke and her walls clamped tight around his thrusting cock. Justin grunted and thrust once as her shoulders trembled, and his release emptied inside her hard and fast.

"I definitely need to leave work early more often," he panted as he reclaimed his breath.

She struggled to breathe at a regular rate and nodded. "I agree."

Justin grinned and covered her mouth in a kiss.

Chapter Ten

Emily Stepped into Portia's salon since it was close to her meeting and hoped her sister could fix her nail. Though it had been over six weeks since she had dropped her off at the wedding planner, things were only mildly better between them.

However, things with Justin were going good. They spent as much time together as possible, and he told her he would off the engagement last night. Insecurity tickled down her spine. He'd been saying that for the previous few weeks, and still, it hadn't happened.

Hopefully soon.

She crossed the threshold and glanced around. She spotted Portia's friend Lucy and smiled. "Is my sister around?"

A thoughtful expression crossed her face. "She was in the stock room a bit ago, but I haven't seen her. She might've gone to lunch." Lucy shrugged. "You might want to check back there."

She nodded and walked toward the back. Emily opened the stock room door and maneuvered around the racks back to where the office was. Her footsteps halted as her sister's moans echoed softly through the door. “God, harder.” A wail left her sister, and it didn’t take a genius to figure out what she was doing. “Oh, God, Adam!” A loud male grunt echoed from behind the office door.

Adam? I thought his name was Henry.

There was silence; the door opened, and her sister stepped out ahead of a guy different from the other day. Her eyes widened, and shock registered on her face. “What are you doing here?” She snapped and narrowed her gaze.

“Silly me thought I’d get my broken nail fixed. I see you’re busy with another client.”

The man darted a glance at Emily and winked. “Great service here. I’ve been coming here for about four years.”

“Four years, wow, good to know.” She plastered a smile and turned to Portia. “Wow, a repeat customer. Makes me wonder how many others you have who are so dedicated.”

“I’ll catch you later,” Adam called as he walked away.

“Have you come to make my life hell, or do you need your nail fixed?”

Emily lifted her middle finger—never so happy that it was the one that had broken. “See, a legitimate reason.”

“I can squeeze you in.”

Emily’s stomach turned. “Have you been screwing him all this time? I mean, during your entire relationship with Justin?”

“What do you care?” Her sister snapped.

"Christ, we've had this talk."

"We have, and you still are making wedding plans while you screw the greater Los Angeles area."

Portia laughed and shook her head. "Justin is a catch. I'm not ruining that."

Part of her wanted to slap her sister stupid. Of course, it would be pointless. She already was. The other part couldn't stand looking at her. "Then, if you don't want to ruin things, you might want to keep your legs together. May I suggest vice grip and duct tape."

"You're such a bitch."

She blinked at the other woman. "Yeah, but I'm smart enough to know a good thing. You know what? Forget about the nail and forget about me. I have to go."

"Remember what I said if you even think of telling anyone." Her sister's tone carried pure venomous rage. "They won't believe you."

Emily's heart sank. Why couldn't Justin see what a lying bitch Portia was? She stormed out of the back room to the salon door and didn't slow down until she hit the sidewalk. Tears threatened, hot, scalding tears of uncertainty and doubt. An intelligent woman would tell the man she loved that his fiancée was cheating.

Her steps halted.

She loved Justin. He was still engaged to Portia. He certainly had the best of both worlds. Her body started to ache, and ringing started in her ears. Emily needed to sit down before she passed out.

She entered the coffee shop and glanced at the man behind the counter. The same one whose car Portia had gotten out of a few weeks before.

What the hell am I going to do?

She was about to slump in a chair when the door opened, and Steve walked in. Disbelief registered on his face. "Emily, what a surprise. How have you been?"

She plastered a smile on her face. "Good, thanks, and you?"

"I've been doing okay, busy with the political campaign." He raked his gaze over her. "You look terrific."

"Thanks."

"Listen, it's the weirdest thing. I actually thought of you today. I was wondering if you wanted to go for dinner tomorrow night. There are some things I wanted to talk to you about." He shook his head. "I know we had a bit of a bad break up, but I'd like to put it behind us."

She blinked at the man she once cared about and thought she loved. "Sure. What time?"

Chapter Eleven

Emily paced her apartment floor and debated what the hell she was doing with her life. Seeing Steve and finding out what he had to say had officially put a twist in her plans. However, every day that passed while Justin still hadn't called the wedding off weighed heavier and heavier on her chest and heart. She was undoubtedly in love with him. However, he wasn't hers to love or even hold.

Yet, they carried on with their relationship secretly while Portia, for the benefit of her family and her fiancé, faked being loving and doting. Meanwhile, when no one was looking couldn't keep her legs together if she tried. A tight knot formed in Emily's stomach. She couldn't keep going like this. So, since Justin had yet to make a move to end the wedding, his actions spoke volumes about where she stood with him.

She struggled not to cry as her cell phone started to ring. She walked over to the table, picked up the device, and glanced at the number.

Mom!

She groaned and answered the call. "Hey, Mom,

what's up?"

"Where are you? You were supposed to meet Portia and me at the bridal shop." She could tell by the tone her mother wasn't happy.

"Is the bride-to-be there, or is she fashionably late like usual?" God, she sounded bitter. Technically, she had every right to be. Her sister was a fake, a phony, and for lack of a better word—a slut.

More like skanky late. Portia's such a tramp.

"Of course she is. She is so excited to get married, and you haven't been supportive." Her mother snorted. "I don't know what's gotten into you."

My sister's fiancé's dick. Thanks for asking.

"So when do you think you will be here?" her mom demanded.

"I won't be. I have work to do and things to care of which are more important."

The front door opened and closed. Justin had arrived, and she might as well have the talk with him now before she lost all courage.

"I'm not happy, Emily. I know Portia will be distraught. I'm beginning to think you're jealous of her."

Oh my god, no.

"No. Actually, I'm not. However, I frankly don't give a damn if Portia pretends to be upset or not. I have no desire to be part of this wedding." Her gaze met Justin's as he walked up the stairs. "Anyway, Mom, good luck with the bridezilla." She ended the call as he stepped over to her.

He leaned in and kissed her lips. She savored the feel since it would be the last one she would have with him. Emily stepped back and met his gaze. "Good timing."

Concern etched across his handsome face. "What's going on?"

She glared at him, and her temper rose to the surface. Anger and hatred filled her, and her heart started to break from the reality of the situation. She was upset with him for not calling off the wedding, concerned with her sister for taking him for granted, and for being a dumbass slut. She was especially angry with herself for loving a completely unavailable man.

"Other than I've had the day from hell?"

He reached to wrap her in his arms, and she stepped away from him. Her heart would never survive this, and she had no one to blame but herself. "I can't keep going like this," she confessed, then turned and met his surprised expression.

More than anything, she wanted to be against his chest and feel his arms around her. Only, it was past the point of no return and would be useless, considering what she had decided. Her blood chilled despite the rage she was feeling.

"Emi, what's wrong?" Greif and worry filled his gaze, and the invisible weight on her shoulders and chest grew heavier.

"I'm having dinner with Steve tomorrow night." The statement fell off her tongue. She didn't think he'd care at this point.

"Why? You two have been broken up for weeks." Justin's gaze darkened. He wasn't happy. Oh well, neither was she.

"Right." Emily struggled to fight back the tears. "And you have no intention of calling off the wedding with my sister. I knew going into this you weren't available. Hell, I'm no better than Portia."

Anger blinked at her from behind his long lashes. "What the hell does that mean? You're nothing like your sister."

She winced and figured she wasn't going to be the one to tell him Portia was a raging slut. If he was too stupid to notice, he wouldn't hear it from her. "Nothing, it doesn't matter." She wanted to cry, but her stupidity had gotten her into this. She was insane for thinking he would leave her perfect sister for someone like her.

Justin shook his head, and frustration etched his handsome face. "Not a day has gone by over the last year or more where I haven't wished I'd met you first."

She wasn't sure if his words were a comfort or a curse. Her heart ached, and she blinked hard to keep tears at bay. "Portia is now shopping with my mother for a wedding dress." She hung her head. "So this leaves me no options. I'm done; I refuse to be second best, especially to someone like her. I'm not waiting around for you to figure out what you want. I think your actions have spoken volumes."

"No, please don't—"

"I'm done if all you want is an affair and to

continue cheating on my sister. Do it with someone other than me. I can't do this anymore." She needed him out of the house before she broke down and cried in front of him.

Sorrow washed over his face. "Emi, I'm in love with you. I have been for well over a year."

Fierce, burning pricks threatened to let the tears spill and take her to resolve. She shook her head. "You have a funny way of showing it, and telling me that before you slapped a ring on my sister's finger would have been a good move."

"I'm trying to make things right now," his tone carried a grief-stricken plea.

"No, you're not, or you would have ended it with my sister. I don't want to be your mistress; I want someone who loves me more than anything, not secondly or on a side note. Obviously, you're not that person."

"Emi..." She could see anguish etched in his handsome features but remained strong.

Tears brushed her lashes. "Please, Justin, go—go be with your fiancée and forget everything we've shared and done."

He shook his head, and for a fleeting second, she thought she saw tears in his eyes. However, without a word, he turned and walked down the stairs. When the front door opened and then closed, she started to cry.

It was all Emily could do not to tell him. She loved him too. It didn't matter now if it had ever mattered at all.

Chapter Twelve

Two days had passed since Justin had left Emily's. His heart ached with every ticking second, and he knew this whole situation was his fault. If he ever hoped to make things right with the woman he loved, he had to end things with Portia. Better sooner than later. He brought his car to a stop in front of the nail salon and sighed. This was probably going to be hell, but right now, he couldn't imagine it being worse than the place he was at currently.

His heart and soul were shredded and in agony.

He turned off the vehicle and exited, setting the alarm. As he approached the door, dread filled him, and he glanced through the window. There, his not-so-innocent fiancée was kissing a man who sure wasn't him. Her arms were laced around the stranger's neck, and he cupped her denim-covered ass in his grip.

He had seen enough. A smile crossed his lips. How could he be so stupid? Reality hit him like a bucket of ice cascading around him. He'd hurt himself and Emily for a woman who had no regard for him. If she had, she wouldn't be kissing the other guy.

God, Emi, what have I done?

He walked back over to his car and climbed in. He wanted to drive to Emily's and beg her to give him another chance. However, she wasn't returning his calls—he highly doubted she would open her door knowing he was on the threshold.

He turned the ignition over and headed to the freeway exit. He needed to talk to Tristan and knew where he could find him. His mind replayed every time he'd confronted Portia over the last three years when he'd heard she was less than loyal. She'd cried, ranted, and promised him she was faithful. Part of him knew it was lies.

He'd made a hell of a mess of his life by not following his instincts. He should call his dad, he always had advice, but Justin couldn't risk hearing how he should stay with the blonde Carter when he loved the brunette one, whose heart he had no doubt broken.

This could've been avoided!

He was so angry with himself, and by the time he pulled into the parking lot of the Crossroads nightclub, he was in worse shape than before. He hurried out of the vehicle and up to the doors. He'd seen Tristan's car outside and knew his friend would have some advice. He also knew Tristan adored Emily and would be downright ruthless, in his opinion. Justin would chance it—and prayed to God his friend had an idea how to win the sexy brunette back.

Tristan was over by the DJ booth and paused as he fixed his gaze on Tristan. "You look like shit, do I dare ask?"

"I fucked up huge," he blatantly admitted as he crossed the wood floor and over to where the other man stood.

"Do I want to know?"

Justin closed his eyes and again reprimanded himself for being a complete idiot. "I ruined everything with Emi. I'm miserable. I broke her heart, I'm sure, and Portia is cheating."

Tristan blinked, and he could tell his friend wasn't impressed. "You fucked things up with Emily?"

"Big time."

Anger flickered over the other man's face. "You're an ass." He shook his head. "Do you know men would give their soul to have a woman adore them and look at them with that much love and affection?" He glanced to the ceiling, then rested his gaze back on Justin. "Me being one of them."

He stared at his friend. "I'm dying inside."

"Good. So you should." Tristan shook his head. "I ran Emily in the search engine. She is a very well-paid woman, but not once would she take a penny from Trevor and me. She did it because she is a good person. A good person is in love with you, and I thought you loved her."

Oh, this was passed an epic fail. "I didn't call off the wedding, afraid I'd look like a total ass for dumping one girl for her sister."

"And your bride is cheating." Tristan scrubbed his face with his hands, then cast a leveled stare. "Do you have proof?"

"Hell yeah, seeing her in another man's arms in the middle of her nail salon while she kissed him, and he groped her ass pretty much-confirmed things." He shouldn't be sarcastic, but he kicked himself even now.

"I've wondered. Portia came in here one night with a guy and said it was her sister's boyfriend. I didn't think anything of it, but she was friendly with a couple of my dancers on ladies' night a few months back." Tristan studied him. "What do you want?"

"I want Emi," he responded. "More than anything in the world."

"Then do us a favor and kick Portia to the curb for good. You can crash at my place." He shook his head. "I should kick your ass; you know that, right?"

Justin smiled at his friend. "I certainly deserve it."

"Hell man, that you do." Tristan put a hand on his shoulder. "Dump Portia, get your ass to my house, and we'll figure out what to do about Emily. She won't listen to you until you do the first two things; that I guarantee you."

He nodded and absorbed his friend's words, knowing damn well he was right.

God, Emi, please give me a second chance.

Chapter Thirteen

Justin sat at the kitchen table, waiting for Portia. The remainder of his stuff was packed in the car. He'd already made two trips to Tristan's and now waited for his soon-to-be ex-fiancée to walk through the door. He didn't know when or if she'd even be home. Justin tried calling Emily again, but her cell had gone to voicemail. He knew he deserved every ounce of whatever cold and silent treatment she dished his way. He admitted now that he screwed up and probably ruined the best thing that ever happened to him.

He heard the key in the lock of the apartment door. Finally, Portia walked in and glanced at him. "I didn't think you'd be here."

He couldn't resist the urge to be sarcastic. "Is that why you decided to show your face, thinking I wouldn't be here?"

Her mouth gaped she scowled. "What is your problem?"

Time for honesty. "You. You're my problem."

"Darling! What does that mean?" She stepped toward where he sat.

He held his hands up, warning her off. "Save it. I

don't want to hear it."

Her gaze narrowed, and her blue eyes held contempt for the first time in a long time in their relationship. "Where the hell do you get off?"

Lately, in your sister.

"Are you cheating on me?" He thought he'd give her the out. "For once in your life, don't lie."

Horror registered on her face. "Emily told you, didn't she? She told you I was having an affair? God, the stupid bitch is so jealous of me!"

"Enough! And don't you ever speak about Emi like that. Your sister has more class than you'll ever possess." Justin's temper hit full swing.

"I hate when you call her that! God, she is nothing special, just another ugly brunette. I'm the thin, petite, beautiful one."

Ugly? Emi? Is she kidding? Wow, who is jealous of who?

"I think you forgot vain on that list and selfish." Why didn't he see this side of her before?

He'd just been blind to it—pretended it didn't exist. Emily was far from ugly; even Tristan thought she was gorgeous. Though his friend always did have a thing for long legs. Long legs and redheads. One day a woman with both qualities would walk into Tristan's life and knock him on his ass. At least Justin had hope. His friend deserved happiness more than anyone he knew.

I'm an idiot!

His heart ached further. He knew what it was like to be completely happy with a woman, and he'd broken their hearts for a woman who'd never be faithful. "I know you're cheating on me with your client, so show some dignity and admit it."

"You weren't around!"

Seriously? How many nights had he sat home alone while she did God knows what with God knows whom?

I broke Emily's heart for this.

Logic kicked him in the gut. He needed a miracle to win the pretty brunette back—the same one having dinner dates with her ex. God, he was dumb, to the point of stupid.

"I'm done, Portia," He finally breathed. "No more us, no more stupid wedding. Nothing. I can't keep this up."

"God! My sister is such a bitch. She has put these crazy thoughts in your head." She batted lashes at him. "I love you."

He saw the woman in front of him in a different light. Tristan was right. She didn't look at him like a woman in love.

Emily did. You were her everything. Way to go! The voice of reason was heartless. Right, but cruel.

"You don't love me. You love you and see me as an opportunity." Saying the words made him nauseous.

"For Christ's sake! We are God damn perfect!" She snapped in a temper and glared at him with an icy stare. "We've got to be one of the best-looking couples to grace the earth."

"No," he sighed and came to a standing position.

"You're unfaithful, and I'm in love with someone else—have been for a long time."

Shock riveted over her features. One time he'd found them pretty. Now he wasn't sure what to think, but if beauty ran more than skin deep, Portia held none. "Are you cheating on me?"

He shook his head and remembered everything he'd shared with Emily. Justin thought of all the reasons why he loved her. It was sad. As he stared at her sister, he couldn't fathom why he was still with her. "I'm done."

"What the hell?"

He sighed and walked to the door. "Keep the ring. I don't want it or you."

"Where the hell are you going?" She raged in a temper, and tears filled her eyes.

Justin didn't care. "Tristan's. Not that it's your business. Have a good life." He turned and reached for the doorknob.

"You never answered me. Are you cheating on me?"

What a seething narcissistic bitch.

He glanced back. "No. The only one I betrayed is me by being with you for as long as I have." Without another word, he pulled open the door and crossed the threshold.

Not once did Justin glance back as he walked to his car, nor did he feel remorse where Portia was concerned. As far as he'd put Emily through, he'd never forgive himself.

Chapter Fourteen

Emily moved like a zombie through her townhouse. She'd have to find a renter to help with the mortgage payments. Glancing at the packed boxes, she again questioned her decision. New York was at the opposite corner of the country from California. However, she needed a fresh start, somewhere different where she wouldn't be reminded for a moment in time that her life had been perfect.

Four days since she'd sent Justin on his way. The knot in her stomach tightened. She didn't want things this way. Justin had called countless times, and every time she tried to reach for the phone like a drug addict, she'd let the voicemail take the call. Sometimes he left a message, which left her in tears. Other times he didn't, and she longed to hear his voice.

The front door opened, and she felt hope. Maybe he'd just stopped by.

"Emily, you bitch!" Her sister's voice echoed through the townhouse as her feet stomped up the steps. "I officially hate you!" her sister spat and crossed the floor to stand directly in front of her.

"Good to know the feeling is mutual." Emily stepped around her sister and picked up a box from the floor.

"Justin is mad at me because he knows I've been having an affair with my client." She all but screamed. "He called off the wedding and moved out. He left me."

Good, about time!

"And this is my fault. How?" She spun around and glared at Portia. God, she held so much contempt for the blonde ungrateful bitch.

Portia snorted and rolled her eyes. "Cut the shit. I know you told him because you knew it would ruin us, and you're so jealous of me."

"Oh, for cripes sake. Grow up, run home, suck Justin's cock, and I'm sure it'll all be better."

"We haven't had sex or anything else in almost two months. He's been distracted, and I've been busy."

"Yes, screwing everything with a dick—except the one you're marrying, has a tendency to be time-consuming." Anger, hurt, and every other emotion raised to the surface like hot lava from the earth's core to the gaping mouth of a volcano. "I'm sure all you have to do is spread your legs, which the good lord knows you do easily enough. Making creamy peanut butter challenging, and Justin will come running back."

"Are you calling me a slut?" Her sister's eyes widened in surprise.

"No, I was trying to be nice by insinuating it and spare the name calling—but slut works." She turned away and walked over to a bookcase. The sooner she packed her stuff and called the movers, the better she'd be.

"Don't walk away from me. Why the hell are you even packing?"

Her last straw of patience snapped. "Because I took a job out of state. Of course, if you paid attention to someone other than yourself, you'd know that."

Her sister's eyes filled with tears. "You can't leave. You must fix this mess you created and get me, Justin, back."

No way. Death first.

"Like hell I do. I never told Justin a damn thing." Regret and heartache consumed her. "I should have, though, how you've not only screwed half of Los Angeles while the two of you have been together, but you have no intention of being faithful until you're good and ready. Isn't that the exact words you used?"

"Is it true?"

Both Emily and Portia turned to the top of the stairs.

Justin stood bouncing his gaze between them. "I knocked, but I thought I'd try the handle when no answer." He paused and inhaled an unsteady breath. "I saw the cars in the drive and knew you were home."

Even though he was genuinely gorgeous, currently, he looked like hell. He hadn't shaved in a couple days, and the dark circles under his eyes revealed he hadn't been sleeping. She wanted to believe he was as miserable as she was but highly doubted it.

"She's lying. She wants me unhappy."

He glared at Portia for a moment. "I don't believe that." He then turned to Emily. "Let's try this again." He stepped closer to where they stood. "Did your sister cheat on me more than once?"

She nodded and glanced to the floor. "Yes."

"You lying bitch!"

Snap!

She lifted her head and stared at the other woman. "I'm not. He can ask Steve. He can ask the wannabe actor guy at the coffee shop next to your salon or probably throw a quarter and hit someone you've screwed."

"Steve? As in your ex-boyfriend?" Surprise reflected in his tone.

Emily met Justin's gaze. "Yeah, screwed him for about two months, about a year into your relationship." She glanced at Portia. "So much for dating him briefly, by the way."

Her sister blinked. "How do you know that?"

"I had dinner with him the other night, and he openly admitted it. Actually, it's a friend of his colleague, with whom I took the job in New York." Again, she faced Justin.

Pain blinked in his blue-grey gaze. "Why are you taking a job out of state?" His gaze remained fixed on her.

"Because I was offered an excellent salary to be an art director at an animation company in New York."

"Why do you care if she moves or not? We need to fix us!"

God! She sounds like a spoiled child in a tantrum.

Justin spun to Portia. "There's nothing to fix. I couldn't marry you even if you weren't cheating on me."

Her sister's eyes widened. "And why the hell not?" She'd gone from whining to angry in record time. Kind of scary, actually.

Justin smiled and shook his head. "Because I'm in love with Emi."

"No, really." She rolled her eyes, tossed her long blonde hair over a shoulder, and rested her gaze again on Justin. "Impossible."

"It's not impossible. Actually, it was quite easy. You're beautiful, but you're not what I want."

Portia's jaw slacked and fell open in shock. "Don't be stupid! Everyone wants me."

"They can have you, and apparently, they have." His blue gaze sparkled. "I want your sister. I have for a while."

Emily blinked at the man who held her heart, and his words sunk in. "Portia, get out."

"No, I'm not finished." She barked similar to a dog with rabies. However, a hissing cobra would have carried less venom than her sister's tone.

"Yes, you are." Emily smiled for the first time in days. "Get the hell out and go whining to mom.

You're damn good at that."

"Why does he get to stay, and I have to leave?" Her sister folded her arms in front of her and scowled.

"Because I'm in love with him—I've loved him for a long time, and I should have said something before he put a ring on your finger." She kept her gaze on the other woman. "I refuse to deny that he and I are a better fit than you and him."

"Oh my god!" Her blue eyes narrowed into little slits as a mortified expression worked across her face. "Did you fuck my fiancé?"

She should lie, but her sister lied enough for an entire twelve-square block radius. "No. However, I had the most incredible sex of my life with him—a lot—and hope to again real soon."

"You're such a slut."

"You would know." The laugh escaped her throat, and Emily suddenly had no remorse. None. "Also, for the record, if you think Steve is better in bed—you're also delusional. Get out of my house Portia, or I'll kick your ass down the stairs and out the door."

"I'll never forgive you for this!" She screamed, then turned to Justin. "And I simply hate you. My parents will never approve of you ditching me for her." She turned and stomped to the stairs. The front door opened and then slammed shut.

Emily closed her eyes and knew hell would be paid with her family. At this moment, she didn't care. She just couldn't keep hurting like this.

Chapter Fifteen

Justin sighed and studied the sexy brunette in front of him. God, how he'd missed her. He stepped closer to her and rested his fingers under her chin. "Look at me."

She lifted her head and met his gaze. Sorrow blinked at him, and his heart broke. "I'm sorry. So very sorry."

Emily was slowly killing him. "The only thing you need to be sorry for is taking a job out of state." He removed the hand beneath her chin and brushed a strand of hair from her pretty face. "I knew the night of the dinner I was marrying the wrong sister."

Her lashes slammed shut, and tears spilled down her cheeks. "You didn't call things off."

"Please don't cry." He gently wiped the tears away and then captured her wrists in his hands. "I want to be with you."

"I should have told you about…." God, which guy in her sister's list of men did she begin with?

He smiled. "I'd heard stories. I confronted Portia about it a couple of times over the years, she denied it, and I didn't have proof." He'd been an idiot. "I didn't want to believe I had chosen so badly, and my parents liked her, or at least, so I thought."

Hesitation filled her eyes. "What do you mean?"

"My dad asked me last night what was wrong, and I told him the truth. I was in love with you and didn't want to marry Portia." His handsome face broke into a smile. "Dad told me I should have picked the smart, beautiful one to begin with instead of the eye candy."

A faint smile dusted her lips. "Your grandma likes me."

Some of the heavy weight eased off his chest. "No, Granny *loves* you. She missed you not being there this week. I should have broken it off with Portia long ago, and I'm sorry for hurting you. We have a New York office. I'll move to be close to you."

Emily removed her hands from his and took a step back. She blinked at him and debated. "You're serious?"

"Very." Never had he felt like his life hung in the balance. "Can you give me a chance to make things up to you? I promise you I'll be faithful. You don't have a reason to believe me, considering I did cheat on your sister." He shook his head and knew for the first time what desperation was.

"True and I..." he could see she was torn and how exhausted she was. "No secrets and no more lies."

"I don't have a reason to." His voice cracked on the last word, and the last thing he wanted was to come undone in front of her. "You're all I want, Emi." He shook his head. "I love the way you are so quick to help people and tell a story with enthusiasm and with such an animated expression. I love how you walk in a room and captivate attention by being you. I even like when you talk with your hands and how you show thoughtfulness and compassion without thinking twice. I'm so in love with you. Please give me a chance to be the man you deserve."

"I can't." She swallowed hard and shook her head. More tears slid down her cheeks.

Justin wanted to wipe them away but couldn't risk her rejecting him. "Emi, I—"

"I can't move to New York. Both families are here, even if mine doesn't speak to me ever again." She flung herself at him and laced her arms tight around his neck. "I like your parents and friends and your grandmother."

His arms enveloped her close to his body. He didn't want to let her go. Not ever. "I love you," he whispered, nuzzling his head down by her ear. Relieved, Justin held Emily in his arms and savored everything about her. From the softness of her hair to the hint of perfume. He had gone for days thinking he would never have the simple luxury of having her in his arms. A mistake he'd never make again.

She glanced up at him and smiled. "I love you too." Emily stretched up and brushed her lips against his.

Relief washed over him, and he claimed her

mouth with tender desire. His hands slid to her ass and tightened his hold on her flesh. He gently squeezed as he pulled her closer. She gasped, and he entered her mouth. His cock stirred and started to stiffen as it pressed against her belly. He slid his hands around to the button of her cut-off shorts and tugged down the metal zipper. The denim slid down her legs to the floor.

"This is going to be the best make-up sex of my life," he whispered.

"Agreed." She stepped out of his arms, pulled his shirt over his head, and tossed it to the floor. "God, you're gorgeous."

He focused his gaze on the scrap of lace that constituted her panties and grinned. "Hold that thought."

Emily blinked. "Where are you going?"

"To lock the front door." He hurried down the stairs, locked the handle and the bolt, then came up the stairs and glanced around. Justin walked down the hall and peeked in the bedroom. She was naked on the bed, and his dick begged to be free. He undid his belt and zipper, then removed his jeans and boxer briefs in a fluid swoop. After stepping out of them, he crossed the floor to the bed and stretched over her.

"What took you so long?"

He chuckled and covered her mouth with his. Her legs parted, and when his arousal brushed against her wet folds, she wiggled beneath him, letting him know she wanted him as badly as he wanted to be buried in her. He groaned against her tongue, entwined with his. The tip of his cock teased at her entrance, and she couldn't hold back any longer. He entered her in a single thrust and was rewarded by a whimper of pleasure against his mouth.

Justin knew he had all night and even the day with her. This might be fast, hard, and intense. However, he knew the woman beneath him was utterly his. Never would he ever doubt her integrity or faithfulness. He lifted his mouth from hers and captured her gaze with his. "I love you, don't ever forget that."

She sighed and bucked her hips, pulling his dick into her wet pussy as far as it would go. "I know."

He grinned and again claimed her mouth as he slowly started working in and out of her. Justin had missed everything about her. His pace picked up speed and momentum. Her body shifted beneath him and her back arched up off the bed, allowing him in deeper. His sac started to ache, and he grew more aroused with every rock of her hips and every soft groan against his tongue. He wanted her to climax before he filled her with his release begging her to let go.

Her mouth lifted from his and her back arched as her hips bucked off the bed. "God! Justin!" She wailed seconds before her body trembled and shook beneath him.

Her wet walls grasped his thrusting dick tighter than ever before and caved to the pleasure. A feral growl left his lips as he slammed deep into her. His balls tightened, and his stomach muscles stiffened as his orgasm pulsed into her hard and fast.

He struggled to breathe. Emily's arms held him tight, and he knew this was where he belonged. "I want to spend the night with you. Tonight and probably the next few decades of them after that."

Her dark eyes sparkled. "Did you already get a place?"

"No. I'm staying with Tristan for now." He scanned her face and grinned. His gaze darted around the room and then again met hers. "I could handle this."

"And I could handle not only you spending nights but waking up with you." She bucked her hips slightly and tightened her muscles around his cock, already stiffening again.

He needed a week in bed with her to make up for all the hurt he'd caused them both. "I'd like that, but first, round two."

She smiled and grasped his shoulders. "And if you're good, I'll even let you have round three."

Justin laughed. "That was the plan." Never would he let her go after knowing what living without her was like. He covered her mouth with his and knew that a life with Emily was where he was supposed to be.

♥

About Kandi Silvers

Born and raised in Las Vegas, Nevada, I still call Sin City home. I've always been a sucker for romance novels and movies, especially romantic comedies. Writing is more than words; it captures slices of characters' lives and shares them with the reader. I firmly believe that heroes and heroines had a life before page one of any story and their past and life experiences made them who they are.

Coming from the southwest, I have a soft spot for cowboys, but I also love suspense, a bit of intrigue, and kick-ass heroines. Of course, there is always the time to slip in a good paranormal. I try to keep my writing diverse and always on the naughty side. Happy reading!

~Kisses,

Kandi

www.kandisilversauthor.com

HER SISTER'S MAN

First Edition 2014
ASIN:

www.ingramcontent.com/pod-product-compliance
Lightning Source LLC
LaVergne TN
LVHW091223150826
845673LV00003B/985

* 9 7 9 8 8 4 7 4 1 9 7 6 5 *